Stone Arch Readers are designed to provide enjoyable reading experiences, as well as opportunities to develop vocabulary, literacy skills, and comprehension. Here are a few ways to support your beginning reader:

- Talk with your child about the ideas addressed in the story.

Each moment spent reading with your child is a priceless investment in his or her literacy life.

Gail Saunders-Smith, Ph.D.

S0-AYO-304

STONE ARCH READERS

are published by Stone Arch Books
A Capstone Imprint
151 Good Counsel Drive, P.O. Box 669
Mankato, Minnesota 56002
www.capstonepub.com

Library of Congress Cataloging-in-Publication Data
   Meister, Cari.
   The shivery shark / by Cari Meister; illustrated by Steve Harpster.
   p. cm. — (Stone Arch readers. Ocean tales)
   Summary: Marco the shark is scared to go to the dentist, but his tooth will not
stop hurting.
   ISBN 978-1-4342-3200-7 (library binding)
   ISBN 978-1-4342-3391-2 (pbk.)
   [1. Sharks—Fiction. 2. Toothache—Fiction. 3. Dentists—Fiction.] I. Harpster,
Steve, ill. II. Title.
PZ7.M515916Sh 2011
[E]—dc22

                               2011000300

                      Art Director: Kay Fraser
                       Designer: Emily Harris
              Production Specialist: Michelle Biedscheid

                      Reading Consultants:

                  Gail Saunders-Smith, Ph.D.
                  Melinda Melton Crow, M.Ed.
              Laurie K. Holland, Media Specialist

       Printed in the United States of America in Melrose Park, Illinois.
                            032011
                          006112LKF11

The SHIVERY Shark

by Cari Meister
illustrated by Steve Harpster

STONE ARCH BOOKS
a capstone imprint

SHARK FUN FACTS

- There are about 375 different kinds of sharks.

- Most sharks never blink or close their eyes.

- A shark can go through 50,000 teeth in its lifetime.

- Some sharks can go without food for a year.

Marco loved gymnastics. He was great at flips.

He was great on the high bar.

But he liked the rings the best.

"He's the best shark I've ever taught," said his coach.

The big sea meet was coming up. Marco wanted to win.

He practiced every day.

But on Tuesday, Marco
wasn't at practice. He missed
Wednesday and Thursday, too.

"I hope he didn't get caught in a net," said his friend Gabe.

"I hope he's not hurt," said his coach.

Marco wasn't caught in a net. He wasn't hurt. He was home in bed with a terrible toothache.

Marco held his jaw with his fin. "OW!" he yelled. "It hurts so bad!"

His dad tried to pull the tooth out.

His mom tried to pull the tooth out.

His sister even tried to pull
the tooth out.

"Sorry, Marco," they said. "We
can't get it."

Marco howled in pain.

Marco's toothache wasn't any better on Friday.

His coach called his mom.

"We need Marco at practice," he said. "The big sea meet is coming up."

Marco was sad. He didn't like
missing practice.

Marco's mom had an idea.

"Let's take you to the dentist," she said.

"To Dr. Gums?" asked Marco. He shivered in fear.

"Yes," said his mom. "He is the best dentist in the sea."

Dr. Gums was the biggest shark in the sea. He was also the scariest. Marco did not want to go and see him.

"He will make you feel better," said his mom.

Marco wasn't so sure.

When they got to the dentist's office, they had to wait. On the counter were large jars full of teeth.

Marco shivered. He tried to hide.

Dr. Gums found him. "Hello!" he said.

Dr. Gums smiled. His teeth were very white. His teeth were very sharp.

Dr. Gums's sharp teeth made Marco shiver. Marco knew that sometimes sharks ate other sharks. He tried to swim away.

"Not so fast, Marco," said
Dr. Gums. "Let's take care of
that tooth."

Dr. Gums had Marco sit in a special chair. He gave Marco special glasses. Even Marco had to agree that they were cool.

Then Dr. Gums got out a special tool. Marco shivered again. "No way!" he yelled. "That will hurt!"

"I'll be fast," said Dr. Gums. "Open wide, like this."

Dr. Gums opened his mouth
really wide. That made Marco
shiver more. But Marco opened
his mouth. In a few seconds,
the tooth was out.

Marco felt much better. He went to practice.

"Glad to have you back," said his coach. "We have lots of work to do before the sea meet."

Marco worked very hard.

And on the day of the meet,
Marco won first place.

The End

STORY WORDS

gymnastics   howled

coach   dentist

toothache   shivered

Total Word Count: 450

WHO ELSE IS SWIMMING IN THE OCEAN?

STONE ARCH READERS   LEVEL 3
THE
BRAVE
PUFFER
FISH
by Carl Meister
Illustrated by Steve Harpster

STONE ARCH READERS   LEVEL 3
The
Fancy
Octopus
by Carl Meister
Illustrated by Steve Harpster

STONE ARCH READERS   LEVEL 3
THE
Hiding
EEL
by Carl Meister
Illustrated by Steve Harpster